To Silas Nathaniel, aka Nestle Snipes
#BarnesBrothersForever
DERRICK BARNES

To my son, Gabriel, and his barber, Mr Reggie
GORDON C. JAMES

CROWN
AN ODE TO THE FRESH CUT

DERRICK BARNES

ILLUSTRATED BY GORDON C. JAMES

WALKER BOOKS

Published in Great Britain 2021 by Walker Books Ltd
87 Vauxhall Walk, London SE11 5HJ

This edition published 2022

10 9 8 7 6 5 4 3 2 1

Text © 2017 Derrick Barnes
Illustrations © 2017 Gordon C. James
First published in the United States by Agate Publishing

The right of Derrick Barnes and Gordon C. James to be identified as author
and illustrator respectively of this work has been asserted in accordance
with the Copyright, Designs and Patents Act 1988

This book has been typeset in Barrio and Akkurat Pro

Printed in China

British Library Cataloguing in Publication Data: a catalogue record for
this book is available from the British Library

ISBN: 978-1-5295-0404-0

www.walker.co.uk

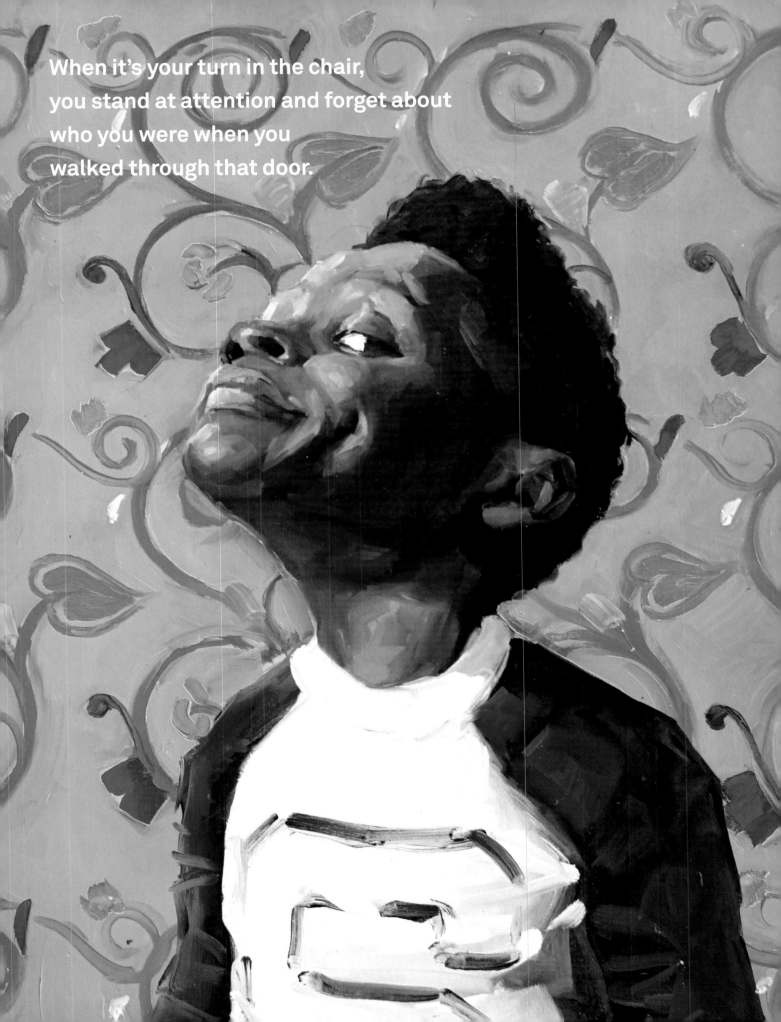

When it's your turn in the chair,
you stand at attention and forget about
who you were when you
walked through that door.

You came in as a lump of clay,
a blank canvas, a slab of marble.
But when my man is done with you,
they'll want to post you up in a museum!

That's my word.

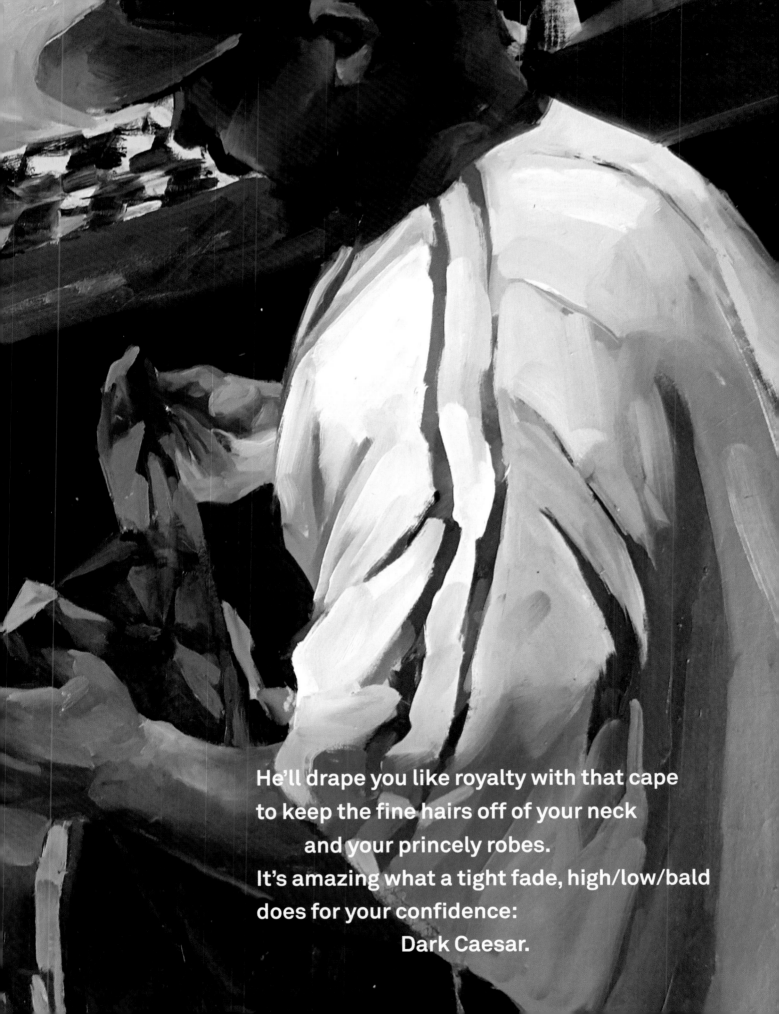

He'll drape you like royalty with that cape
to keep the fine hairs off of your neck
and your princely robes.
It's amazing what a tight fade, high/low/bald
does for your confidence:
Dark Caesar.

Who knows? You might just smash that geography exam tomorrow and be top of your class.
A fresh cut does something to your brain, right?
It hooks up your intellectual.

You're a star.
    A brilliant, blazing star.
Not the kind that you'll find on a sidewalk in Hollywood.
Nope. They're going to have to wear shades
when they look up to catch your shine.

He'll lean you back in the chair,
dab that cool shaving cream on your forehead,
and then craft a flawless line with that razor –
slow, steady, surgical.
    It frames your swagger.

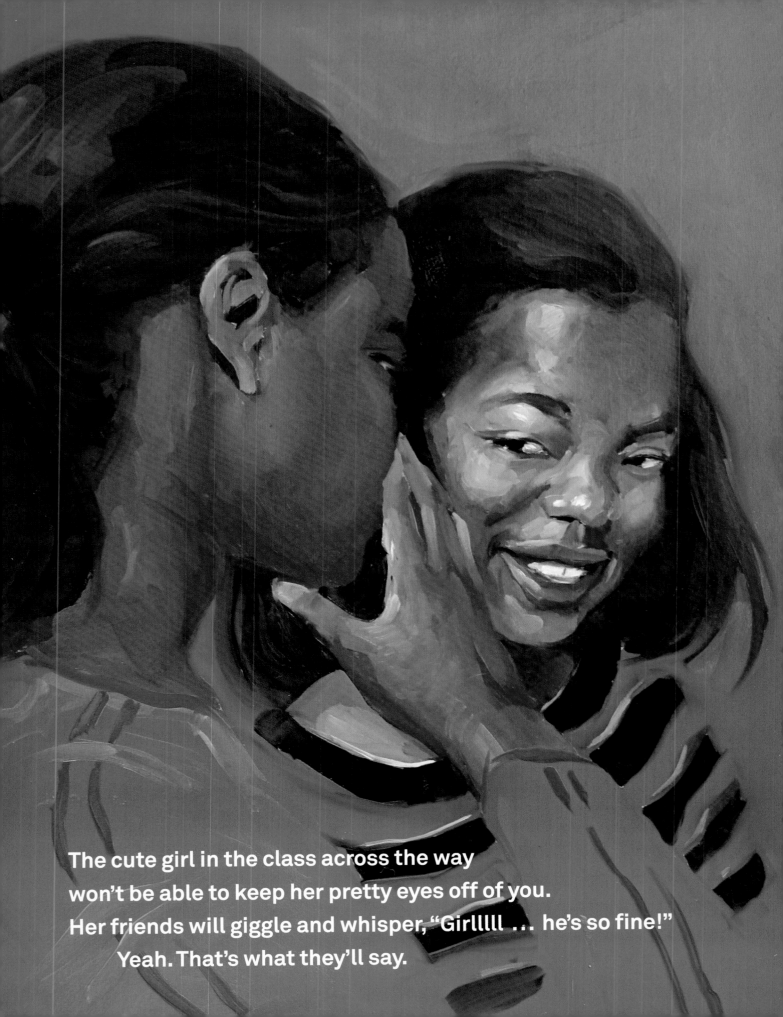

The cute girl in the class across the way
won't be able to keep her pretty eyes off of you.
Her friends will giggle and whisper, "Girlllll … he's so fine!"
Yeah. That's what they'll say.

The whole school will be seasick from the rows and rows of ripples.
You'll have more waves on your head than the Atlantic Ocean.
(Shout out to my do-rag and patience.)

There's a dude to the left of you
with a faux-hawk, deep part, skin fade.
He looks presidential.
Maybe he's the CEO of a tech company that
manufactures cool.
He's a boss.
That's how important he looks.

Dude to the right of you looks majestic.
There are thousands of black angels
waiting to guide and protect him
as soon as he steps a foot out that door.
That's how important he looks.

There's a dude standing in the mirror that can't get over
the masterful designs crafted on the side of his dome.
Everywhere he goes, people will ask for his autograph.
    He looks that FRESH!
He looks like he owns a few acres of land on Saturn.
Maybe there's a river named after him on Mars.
    He looks that important.

There are two dudes, one with locs, the other with cornrows, and a lady with a butterscotch complexion, and all they want is a "shape up", "tapered sides", "a trim" and a crisp but subtle line.
And sometimes in life, that's all you ever need.
A crisp but subtle line.

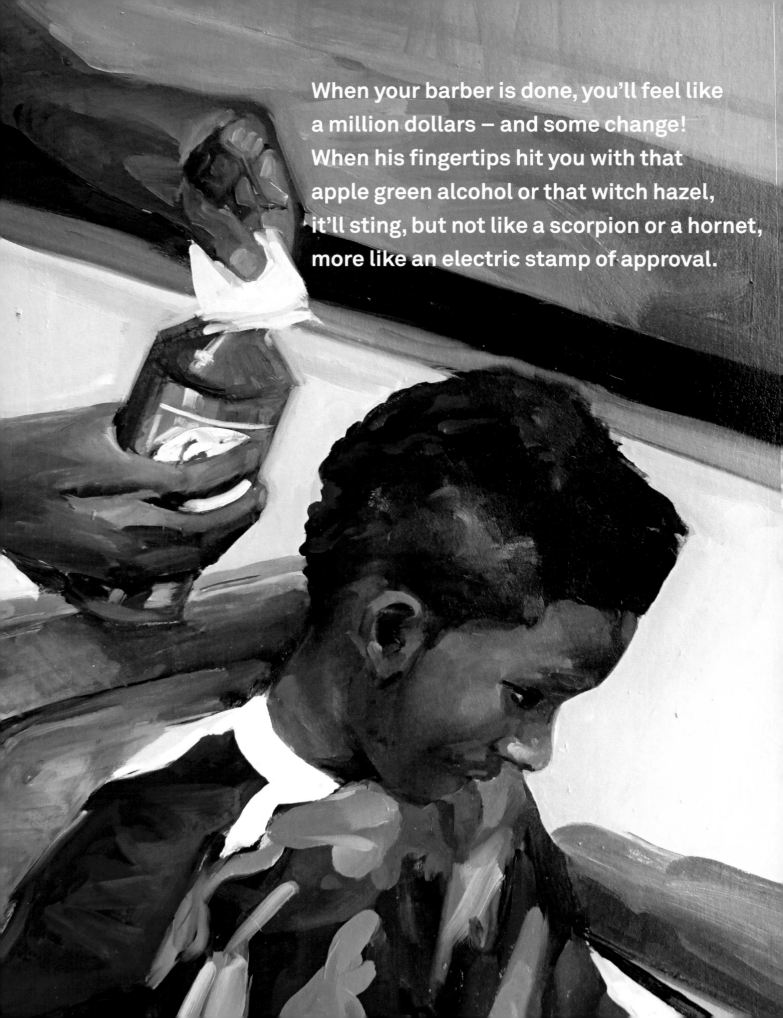

When your barber is done, you'll feel like a million dollars – and some change! When his fingertips hit you with that apple green alcohol or that witch hazel, it'll sting, but not like a scorpion or a hornet, more like an electric stamp of approval.

And when you see the cut yourself,
in that handheld mirror,
you'll smile a really big smile.
That's the you that you love the most.
That's the you that wins – everything.
That's the gold medal you.

Every person in the shop will rise to their feet
and give you a round of applause
for being so FLY!
Not really … but they'll look like they want to.
You'll see it in their eyes.

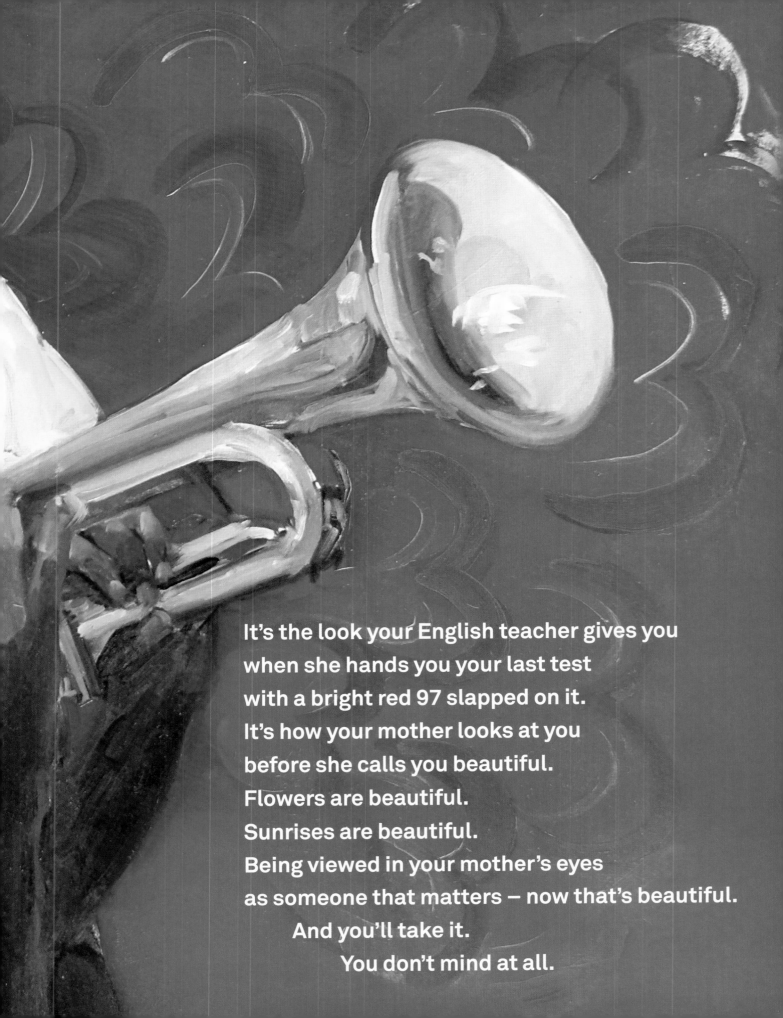

It's the look your English teacher gives you
when she hands you your last test
with a bright red 97 slapped on it.
It's how your mother looks at you
before she calls you beautiful.
Flowers are beautiful.
Sunrises are beautiful.
Being viewed in your mother's eyes
as someone that matters — now that's beautiful.
And you'll take it.
You don't mind at all.

Finally, he'll remove your cape, then swipe you down with a brush made from a golden horse tail.

You'll put the money in his hand
without even expecting change back.
Tip that man!
Tip that man!
It was worth it. It always is.

Hello, world...

You know why?
Because you'll leave out of "the shop",
every single time, feeling the exact same way...

Magnificent.
Flawless.
Like royalty.

A NOTE FROM THE AUTHOR

Mr Tony was my barber in the sixth grade. To get to his chair, I rode the Prospect southbound Metro bus to 63rd Street in Kansas City every Thursday, the day of the week my mother would leave eight dollars on the kitchen table so that I could get my hair cut. Walking out of that shop, I never felt like the same kid that went in. I couldn't wait for Friday morning so that Carmella Swift, my girlfriend, could see how perfect my box was shaped up. I knew she'd bug out about the two parts on the right side of my head, which, in my mind, made me look like Big Daddy Kane. There was no way she'd resist my ruler-straight hairline, a precise frame for my smiling, brown, 11-year-old face. That fresh cut made you more handsome. It made you smarter, more visible and more aware of every great thing that could happen in your world.

With this offering, I wanted to capture that moment when black and brown boys all over America visit "the shop" and hop out of the chair filled with a higher self-esteem, with self-pride, with confidence and an overall elevated view of who they are. The fresh cuts. That's where it all begins. It's how we develop swagger, and when we begin to care about how we present ourselves to the world. It's also the time when most of us become privy to the conversations and company of hardworking black men from all walks of life. We learn to mimic their tone, inflections, sense of humor, and verbal combative skills when discussing politics, women, sports, our community and our future. And really, other than the church, the experience of getting a haircut is pretty much the only place in the black community where a black boy is "tended to" – treated like royalty.

Crown: An Ode to the Fresh Cut focuses on the humanity, the beautiful, raw, smart, perceptive, assured humanity of black boys/sons/brothers/nephews/grandsons, and how they see themselves when they highly approve of their reflections in the mirror. Deep down inside, they wish that everyone could see what they see: a real life, breathing, compassionate, thoughtful, brilliant, limitless soul that matters – that desperately matters. We've always mattered. *– Derrick Barnes*